T.A. BARRON

The Day the Stones Walked

A Tale of Easter Island

illustrated by WILLIAM LOW

PHILOMEL BOOKS

Some days are large as the starlit sea. Some days are small as a rock lizard's eye. And some days are both at once—like the day the stones walked.

S alt wind slapped my face as I brought home my catch—two sea urchins, wrapped in a banana leaf, and a black crab, stuck on the point of my spear. I thought Mala would be proud of me. But she looked right past me at the strange gray-green clouds beyond the shore.

"Those clouds . . . ," she muttered, dropping her favorite bird-bone needle and the *tapa* cloth she was mending. "Just like the ones I saw as a child, right before the Great Wave."

I looked up at the sky. It was one thing to hear the spirit-singers, who were always expecting trouble, predict a Great Wave. But it was another thing to hear it from Mala.

"I must warn the village! But you—go to your father. Tell him to flee, like everyone else, to the highest caves!"

I did not have to ask where he was. Up with the *moai*, the old stone statues on the ridge. Still carving, as always.

"Run, Pico!"

I ran up the ridge of Rano Raraku, but not very fast. After all, this was probably just another storm from the sea. How could it be a Great Wave? Hadn't I just waded in the sea, in waves bluer than a bluefish and calmer than a sleeping clam?

All around me now, great chins jutted, dark eyes peered, and harsh brows loomed, on bodies that stood six or seven times taller than me. Some leaned sideways, others forward—as if they were walking, striding on the slope.

But I knew the truth. They could not move. Only in the old stories did the *moai* come alive and walk, to help our people in times of trouble. But nobody believed those stories anymore. Nobody—except my father.

When I found him, his brown back gleamed with sweat, right down to his *hami*. He was carving the long, straight edge of a *moai*'s ear. Hearing my gusty breaths, he stopped and set down his *toki*.

"My Pico. You have come to watch?" He patted the stone's enormous chin. "This one is almost done—almost alive. I can feel it. Someday, if our people need help, he will stir. And then he will walk."

I wasn't listening. "There's a storm, Pala! Maybe a Great Wave! Mala says we should go"—I nodded toward the higher ridge on the other side of the island—"up there, to the caves."

He frowned. "So you did not come to learn how to carve?"

I shook my head. Why did he never teach me how to build a boat or hunt the octopus at night, like other fathers? I leaned back against the stone— which felt warm, but only from the sun. "Stones are not alive, Pala."

His eyes, black as a sea tern's, studied me. "Not now, my Pico. But when the time is right, and the *mana* spirit flows from the mountain—"

"Pala, please! I know the truth. Everyone does but you. They are only stones."

"They are our ancestors. Our protectors. They watch over our people—yes, even now." His eyes brewed storms of their own. "Leave me, my Pico. I have work to do. You go hide with the others."

I turned and ran down the slope, heading for the trail that led across the island and then up to the caves. "Stupid old man," I growled. The *moai* seemed to bend lower, listening.

But why should I care? They could not hear me.

Suddenly I came to the ledge above the shore. I saw the clouds again. But they looked different now—like dark, shadowy waves slapping the sky. And below, where real waves should have been, I saw nothing.

Nothing at all! The shallows were empty, and dry as a *moai*'s chin.

A tern screeched above me. Then, in the distance, I saw a wave. Taller than any wave I'd ever seen, taller than the village, maybe taller than the mountain. Rushing in to shore!

I spun around. Must warn Pala!

Back up the mountain I ran, higher and higher, leaping over rocks and bushes. Behind me I heard the rising roar of the Great Wave.

I tripped and fell, twisting my knee. Though I got up again, my leg felt heavy as stone.

Up through the *moai* I staggered, as the roar grew louder. My knee ached, my chest pounded. I fell again, knocking my head, and for a moment I just lay there, dazed. Somehow, I forced myself to stand.

Then the wave slammed into the shore,
so hard that the ground shook and spray
rained down on my back.

Water! I glimpsed Pala higher on the slope—but when
I called to him, the wave swallowed my words. The sea
surged over me, foaming, bashing me with rocks and
shells, whipping me with shreds of kelp.

I tried to swim, but only sank, flailing like a netted fish. Water poured down my throat, flooded my lungs. There was nothing to grab—nothing to hold.

Then I felt something hard. A *moai*! I grabbed hold, clinging to stone, clinging to life.

Half drowned, I barely held on. All at once, the statue seemed to shift beneath me. To lift me higher. And then—

To walk.

Beyond the rushing waters, I thought I heard the sound of great feet trudging, pounding, striding on the slope.

And voices,
    deeper than the sea itself,

chanting songs of stone.

Spirit-singers still tell the tale of that day, when the sea reached the highest stones of Rano Raraku. It was a day both large and small in my memory—large as the long wet hug from my father, and small as the spark that he saw in my eye.

It was the day the stones walked.

AUTHOR'S NOTE

For hundreds of years, the great stone faces of Easter Island have intrigued explorers and researchers. Who made them? How? And why? And one more puzzle has always sparked my imagination: What happened on that final day, when the very last carver set down his tools?

No one can say for certain—except perhaps the stones.

This place, you see, is the world's most remote inhabited island. It lies over 2200 miles west of South America, in the middle of the Pacific Ocean. Ancient people called it Te Pito Te Heanua, "the belly button of the world," while modern people have dubbed it "the loneliest island on Earth." Both names fit well, for you could sail almost 1200 miles in any direction without sighting a seaport, a village, or a lighthouse. The mystery of the island's *moai* is rivaled only by the mystery of how seafarers ever found it at all, more than fifteen centuries ago.

The *moai*, carved by hand from volcanic basalt, are truly immense. Some of them stand over thirty feet high and weigh more than eighty tons. But even for these huge monoliths, the rare but deadly Great Waves—tsunamis—are a danger. The most recent tsunami to hit Easter Island (triggered by a violent earthquake in Chile) struck in 1960, and toppled several *moai*. And as the world saw on December 26, 2004, tsunamis are both terribly sudden—and terribly violent. The disaster of that day killed thousands of people in Indonesia, Sri Lanka, and Thailand, plus hundreds more in India, Malaysia, the Maldives, Myanmar, and Somalia.

We may never know what really happened on that final day on Easter Island, when the people finally stopped carving *moai*. But there is strong evidence that the collapse of their society, which was Polynesia's most advanced megalithic culture until the 1600s, resulted from a self-inflicted environmental disaster.

Deforestation brought about their doom—more subtly than a Great Wave, but just as disastrously. People just cut too many trees too quickly. In doing so, they ultimately destroyed the ecological and social health of what must have been a glorious place to live.

For centuries after people arrived, a rich subtropical forest covered the island. The world's largest palm tree grew there. And for the people, the word *rakau* meant both "tree" and "wealth." It's easy to see why, since almost everything they needed came from the trees: food to eat, timber to carve their tools and ocean canoes, bark to make clothing, fronds to roof their homes, firewood to cook meals, as well as material for ropes and sleds to move their *moai*.

But as the trees disappeared, so did the island's native birds and animals—and the people's ability to survive as they had for centuries. All this poses questions for us, questions that are both urgent and frightening. Will we, who live on the bigger island called Earth, learn from the experience of Easter Island? Or will we make the same mistake on a much larger scale?

When I traveled to Easter Island with my wife, Currie, it was to fulfill a lifelong dream of seeing those great carved faces. But I had no idea that the stones themselves would tell me a story. It was inspired partly by old island legends, partly by our own experience of finding an ancient carving tool, and partly by something else—something from the stones.

T. A. B.

TO CURRIE, WHO SHARED THE DREAM . . . AND THE JOURNEY —TAB

TO MAX GINSBURG, IRWIN GREENBERG AND MY FRIENDS

AT THE EARLY MORNING CLASS —WL

Patricia Lee Gauch, Editor

PHILOMEL BOOKS
A division of Penguin Young Readers Group. Published by The Penguin Group.
Penguin Group (USA) Inc., 375 Hudson Street, New York, NY 10014, U.S.A.
Penguin Group (Canada), 90 Eglinton Avenue East, Suite 700, Toronto, Ontario, Canada M4P 2Y3 (a division of Pearson Penguin Canada Inc.).
Penguin Books Ltd, 80 Strand, London WC2R 0RL, England.
Penguin Ireland, 25 St. Stephen's Green, Dublin 2, Ireland (a division of Penguin Books Ltd.).
Penguin Group (Australia), 250 Camberwell Road, Camberwell, Victoria 3124, Australia (a division of Pearson Australia Group Pty Ltd).
Penguin Books India Pvt Ltd, 11 Community Centre, Panchsheel Park, New Delhi - 110 017, India.
Penguin Group (NZ), Cnr Airborne and Rosedale Roads, Albany, Auckland 1310, New Zealand (a division of Pearson New Zealand Ltd).
Penguin Books (South Africa) (Pty) Ltd, 24 Sturdee Avenue, Rosebank, Johannesburg 2196, South Africa.
Penguin Books Ltd, Registered Offices: 80 Strand, London WC2R 0RL, England.

Text copyright © 2007 by Thomas A. Barron.
Illustration copyright © 2007 by William Low.

Published simultaneously in Canada.   Manufactured in China by South China Printing Co. Ltd.
Design by Semadar Megged. The illustrations were rendered on the computer using Adobe Photoshop. The text is set in 14.5 Point Thesis TheSerif.

Library of Congress Cataloging-in-Publication Data
Barron, T. A.   The day the stones walked / T. A. Barron ; illustrated by William Low.   p. cm.
Summary: Pico does not believe the old stories that say the moai, the stone statues of his village, come alive and protect the people in time of trouble, until a great wave comes and he is in grave danger. Includes facts about tsunamis, Easter Island, and the effects of deforestation.
[1. Statues—Fiction. 2. Tsunamis—Fiction. 3. Easter Island—History—Fiction.] I. Low, William, ill. II. Title.
PZ7.B27567Day 2007   E]—dc22   2006024881
ISBN 978-0-399-24263-2
1 3 5 7 9 10 8 6 4 2
First Impression